Only
You

M. Worthy

ISBN 13: 978-0692736920
ISBN 10: 0692736921

Chapter One

Samantha slammed the desk drawer shut. *Screw you, Jake Forester. Who needs your sorry ass, anyway? As far as I'm concerned, you and that bleached blonde, fake boobs, airhead Marianne can <u>have</u> each other.* The partitions dividing her tiny cubicle from the rest of her colleagues in the office rattled from the force.

"Hey, Sam! I don't know what your problem is, but I'm trying to get some work done over here," Abigale shouted from the next cubby.

"Sorry," Samantha replied sullenly. *Sure. It's easy to get your work done when your life is fucking perfect.*

Abigale had been the one to train Sammi when she first started at the law firm of Matheson, Matheson, Barton,

M. Worthy

and Colbert. Like Sam, Abigale was a paralegal and legal assistant to the attorneys in the firm. The major differences between the two women were their ages and their level of satisfaction with, not only their jobs, but their lives in general.

Samantha knew that Abigale was in her late thirties—close to ten years older than Sam. Abby had married her high school sweetheart not long after they'd both finished their education. Her husband, Edward, was some kind of an engineer, so between the two of them they made a comfortable living. Of course, the couple had the requisite two children – a boy and a girl. It would be impossible to miss that fact, considering the plethora of family photos and pictures of lopsided houses surrounded by flowers and sunshine plastered all over the walls of Abby's cubicle.

In spite of the differences in their ages and lifestyles, Samantha and Abby had become good friends. Still, Abigale's picture perfect life got to Sammi sometimes—especially lately.

Some people have all the luck, Sam grumbled to herself. When she first started at Matheson and Matheson, she thought her life was destined to follow the same path as

Only You

Abigale's. Jacob Forester was the love of her life. They'd met when she was at UCLA. He had these *amazing* green eyes, and he wore his dark hair long on top and shaved close to his head on the sides. Samantha's heart had skipped a beat the first time she saw him. When he started talking to her at the frat party she'd gone to with her roommate, Kaitlyn, Sammi was so nervous she could hardly speak.

Before the party was over, Jacob Forester had asked, and Samantha had given him her phone number. She figured he was just being polite, and she'd never hear from him again. After all, he was an upperclassman, a star on the football team, and a member of Sigma Chi, one of the best fraternities on campus. Without any effort at all, he could have practically any girl at school he wanted. On the other hand, Samantha figured she'd be lucky to attract the biggest nerd with the thickest glasses and the most zits on campus. Why Jacob Forester had bothered with her at all was almost incomprehensible to her.

It was an absolute surprise when he *did* call a couple of days later. For their first date, he'd taken her out to dinner at a popular Italian restaurant. When the waiter slipped and

M. Worthy

mostaccioli and meatballs spilled into her lap, Jake had sprung from his chair and helped her clean the mess from the front of her blouse. When his hands brushed across her breasts, she was lost. They'd skipped dinner and gone back to his room where they had sex for the first time. Jacob had come rather quickly, but Samantha didn't mind. Being with Jake was a privilege, and she didn't take it for granted. Not only did she do his homework, she opened her legs for him any time he wanted.

Jacob got off too many times to count during their weekends together. Sammi ... not so much. She never had an orgasm when she was with Jake, but neither she nor Jake seemed to mind. Who needed orgasms when you had Jacob Forester? For Samantha, there was no doubt—it was love. *When he took my body, he stole my heart at the same time.*

Opening the drawer she'd just slammed shut, Samantha pulled out the picture that had caused her violent reaction. "We were so good together," she whispered to the smiling couple in the frame.

For the last two and a half years, they were practically inseparable. After that first night, she stayed with

Only You

him every weekend and sometimes during the week. They'd moved into an apartment close to campus the following fall. In addition to doing any and all assignments Jake might have, she cooked and cleaned—did all of his laundry along with her own. Whatever he needed. Whatever he wanted. Samantha would do almost *anything* for him. Jacob Forester was the love of her life.

Samantha never missed a single one of his games—always sitting in the same seat so he could spot her easily whenever he made a spectacular play. She'd scream his name, jump up and down and wave her arms like an idiot. If the game didn't go the way he wanted it to, Sam was the one who was always there to bolster his ego.

"It wasn't your fault, Jake" was her favorite line, and Jacob seemed to love hearing it. From there it would vary depending on the play that had gotten fouled up. "That guy came out of *nowhere.* Not even the best professional quarterback in the world could have avoided that interception."

"Do you really think so?"

M. Worthy

"I don't just *think* so, I *know* so," Samantha would reassure him.

They had a ritual after every game. When they got home, her hero would get his choice. He liked Samantha to give him blow jobs, but he was always asking her to let him come in her mouth.

"Come on, Sam. If you really loved me like you say you do, you'd do it."

"You know I would if I could, Jake." She would stroke his cock for what seemed like hours while he'd lay with his back propped up against the pillows on the bed.

"Geez, Sam. You know I need more than just your hand to get off. Suck on it."

While her hand continued to slide up and down, Samantha would dutifully bob her head on his hard dick. "Ummm," she murmured. His eyes were closed, and he was moaning in ecstasy. He never seemed to notice that she was rolling her eyes and wondering *How much longer do I have to do this?*

"*I'm gonna come.* Suck harder, Sammi. Come on, baby, swallow it. *Please.*"

Only You

As much as she wanted to please him, she almost threw up the one time she tried. Ever since then, their routine was he'd jerk himself off while she played with his balls. Then she'd let him come on her face.

"Thanks, babe. That felt good. I'll give you a kiss after you get cleaned up."

Most of the time, he'd be snoring by the time she'd returned from the bathroom.

After all she'd done for him, Jake had broken her heart by having sex with that slut, Marianne. Samantha had caught the two of them in bed together over eight months ago.

Sam just stood there and watched as the bitch sucked on Jake's dick like it was the sweetest lollipop on the planet.

"Yeah, baby, suck it. Suck it dry." Samantha had heard Jake utter those words a zillion times.

This time a female voice that wasn't Sam's answered breathily between licks. "You bet I will, Jacob. I can't wait to taste your cum. Give it to me; baby. I'm going to swallow every drop."

M. Worthy

As Samantha walked out of the room, she heard the love of her life moan in ecstasy, "Yesssss! I'm coming. Yessss!"

Sam only went back to the apartment once to get her personal belongings. Jacob had shown no remorse. He'd actually *blamed* it all on Samantha.

Even though it was now coming up on a year since that terrible day, it felt like only yesterday. Samantha had learned her lesson. No way was she *ever* going to give her heart away like that again.

Chapter Two

The aroma of coffee roused Samantha from her memories. When she looked up, Damien Williams was standing at the edge of her cubicle.

"I fixed it just the way you like it," he said. "Lots of cream and no sugar." Damien set the Styrofoam cup on her desk and reached into his pocket. "Even brought you some of that sweetener you like." He laid several packets of Truvia next to the coffee. "You okay?"

"Yeah. I'm fine. Thanks for asking." *Why couldn't I have fallen for a guy like Damien?* Okay, he was black, but he was actually a very attractive guy. No, he didn't have the muscular build that Jake had spent hours working on at the gym. Damien was more slender, but not skinny. He wore his black hair buzzed on the sides—short and curly on top. Samantha took a moment to look into his eyes for the first time. They were so brown, they were almost black. She had

M. Worthy

never really noticed before, but now she saw the soft warmth in those eyes and noted the gentleness in his smile. "Did you go to the shelter this weekend?" she asked. Everyone knew that when he wasn't working, Damien donated as much time as he could to the local animal shelter.

He shook his head. "Couldn't. My mom needed some help. Since I'm the only one who lives close by, I'm the one she calls." He shrugged. "I don't mind. She sure sacrificed a lot for me and my brothers and sisters."

Samantha didn't know much about Damien. Sometimes she was assigned to assist him on his cases, but that was about all. She wasn't even sure of his age. She figured he was still pretty young—probably not much older than she was.

Office gossip had it that he was being considered for a junior partner position. Damien was one of the few blacks at the firm. He was known for his hard work and was well liked by the partners as well as everyone else in the office.

"I'm sure she appreciates your help." Sammi smiled slightly. She felt a little self-conscious as she fingered the edges of the frame she held in her lap.

Only You

"What's that?" he asked.

"Oh, nothing. Just an old picture. I should probably get rid of it." Now it was her turn to shrug.

"Old boyfriend, huh?" He grinned.

How come I never noticed how great his smile is? "Uh ... well."

"That's okay. I'm being nosy. Forget I asked."

"No. It's all right. Really. It *is* an old boyfriend, and it's long past the time I should have gotten rid of this thing." Samantha reached over and dropped the frame into the trash can next to her desk. "There," she said while swiping her hands together.

Damien smiled again. "I didn't come over here *just* to deliver you a cup of coffee."

Samantha pushed out her lower lip in a pout. "No? Gosh, I thought maybe you had a little office crush on me or something." *Oh, God, why did I say that?*

"Maybe, but that's not why I'm here either."

"Then why *are* you?"

M. Worthy

One of the partners asked me to do some fairly extensive research on a big case he's working on—interview some people, dig a little deeper. That sort of thing. It's going to require being out of town for a few days. I need someone to go with me—take notes, keep things organized. You know what I mean."

"And?"

"And they want *you* to go with me. Is that all right with you?"

Suddenly Samantha's heartbeat sped up dramatically. "Sure. No problem. Where are we going and when do we leave?"

"Tomorrow. We're going to New York, and we leave in the morning. Can you be ready by seven? A cab will pick you up and take you to the airport. I'll meet you there."

Damien smiled to himself as he walked away from Sam's desk. There was no reason for her to know that he'd *asked* to have Samantha Mason accompany him on the trip

That is one <u>hot </u>white chick. She's got a great ass and big tits. I'm sure looking forward to fucking the hell out of her

Only You

sweet pussy. And I can think of a few other places I'm going to enjoy shoving this bad boy into too, he thought as he mentally patted the front of his trousers.

I wonder if she's ever had a black cock. Well, she's going to real soon, and she's going to love it.

Chapter Three

Samantha had the most erotic dreams ... *ever.* When she awoke the next morning she could feel an unfamiliar tingle between her legs. *What's wrong with me?* In her sleep, she'd seen dark black eyes and chocolate skin. The look in those eyes was filled with lust.

Shaking her head in an attempt to clear her mind of the dream, she stripped off her flannel pjs. Before stepping into the shower, she stood naked in front of the full length mirror mounted to the back of her bathroom door.

Not too bad, she thought. Jake had always liked her tits. He said her big boobs helped balance out her big ass. Sam turned her body to look at her firm and bouncy backside. Her ex-boyfriend had often told her she must have some African American or Latino blood in her heritage somewhere. He claimed that was the only way to account for her rounded hips and plump derriere. Jake hadn't liked her

Only You

ample behind. He often teased her about it. Consequently, she was quite self-conscious regarding that particular area of her anatomy, and did everything she could to hide it. *Maybe Damien likes a big booty. Holy crap! Where are these crazy thoughts coming from?*

Quickly, Samantha stepped into the shower. Squirting body wash onto her shower puff, she started rubbing the foam across her chest. As she smoothed the scented soap over her breasts, her nipples hardened. Without thinking, she began rolling one of the stiff tips between her thumb and forefinger. Closing her eyes and leaning her head back under the spray, she imagined dark hands with light palms taking the place of her own. Her hand seemed to move downward of its own volition. A moan escaped from her lips as her middle finger circled around the tight nub between her thighs. Samantha's legs started shaking, and she stopped herself. It was the closest she'd ever come to an orgasm.

Damien was standing just inside the door of the terminal marked departing flights for Delta. He watched as Samantha stepped out of the cab. When she turned to pay the driver

M. Worthy

who retrieved her carry-on bag from the trunk, he admired the view. Even the hip length coat she wore couldn't hide her curves. *Um. Um. Um. That is one sweet ass.*

She walked through the doors, and a smile lit her face when she saw him. "Good morning, Damien," she said. "I'm not late, am I?"

"Right on time. I thought we'd go through security together. You're registered for TSA's PreCheck, aren't you?"

"Sure am. It's worth it, even though I don't fly that often." She chuckled slightly. "Patience isn't exactly my strong suit."

"Me neither. I'm more of a 'Let's cut to the chase and get down to business' kind of guy." *And that's exactly what I plan on while we're together.*

Samantha looked at him quizzically. "Penny for your thoughts."

"Later. We'll have a chance to talk more on the plane." Casually, he took her hand. "Let's go." Her hand remained in his as they walked toward their gate.

Only You

The tingle Samantha had been feeling between her legs seemed to intensify with her hand linked firmly with Damien's. The sensation was unfamiliar, but not unpleasant. It started almost as soon as she learned of her upcoming trip to New York with Damien and hadn't gone away since.

Surreptitiously she observed their hands. His was large—his fingers long and slim, making her hand look small and pale in contrast. He walked slightly in front of her, so the appearance was more like he was pulling her along, rather than holding hands with her. Samantha liked the feel of his skin. It was soft and smooth—definitely the hands of a professional. His nails were short and manicured perfectly.

I bet he knows <u>exactly</u> how to use those beautiful fingers to pleasure a woman. She tripped over her own feet falling forward into Damien. He moved quickly, dropping her hand and stopping her fall by grasping her firmly around the waist.

"You okay?" he asked as his hands moved up her arms.

M. Worthy

Samantha gulped and stared into his eyes. Licking her lips, she managed to blink and mumble, "I'm fine. Just clumsy, I guess."

"Don't say those kinds of things about yourself, Samantha. We all get tripped up every once in a while. I'm just glad I was here to catch you. That could have been a nasty fall."

A warm glow seemed to suffuse Sam's body at his thoughtful comments and solicitousness. She couldn't speak. Nodding her head, she smiled in appreciation.

Chapter Four

The flight to New York was relatively short and uneventful. Samantha and Damien drank coffee and discussed the particulars of the trip. He briefed her on what the partners expected them to accomplish while they were out of town.

When they arrived at the hotel and checked in, Samantha was not surprised to find that her room was right next door to Damien's. They stood next to each other in the hallway as they inserted their key cards into the locks.

"Want to meet in the lobby in about twenty minutes?" he asked. "Will that give you enough time to do whatever you need to do?"

"Twenty minutes is more than enough," Sam replied. "All I have to do is hang up a couple of things so they don't get too wrinkled. I'm wearing what I have on."

M. Worthy

"Good. I was hoping you weren't one of those high maintenance kind of girls," Damien replied with a grin before disappearing into his room.

Samantha stepped into her hotel room and looked around. There was a small couch with a coffee table in front of it, and a desk with room for her to work from the computer she'd brought with her. It wasn't until after she threw her suitcase on the end of the large king-sized bed that she noticed the door adjoining her room to Damien's.

Her breath caught in her throat as she stared at the door. *Did he know these were adjoining rooms?* In spite of the warmth of the air, her nipples tightened. Once again, she noted the sensation between her legs. It seemed to grow stronger every time she thought about Damien Williams.

Damien chuckled to himself as he imagined Samantha's reaction to the door connecting their rooms. He was certain they'd only need one of the king-sized beds. But booking only one room would have been way too presumptuous of him.

It was almost too bad they'd had to take a morning flight. On the other hand, the anticipation leading up to their

Only You

evening together was going to make it all that much more exciting.

He hung his suits and shirts in the closet and put the box of condoms into the drawer next to the bed. There were already two in his wallet and a few more in the pocket of his jacket ... just in case they ended up in her room instead of his. *This* was an evening that was going to require *several* of those foil packets.

Smiling to himself, Damien left his room and walked to the elevator. He was just about to step in when he heard a voice call out, "Hold that for me please." He did as she asked. Samantha stepped into the small space. "Thanks," she whispered.

His gaze paused only slightly at her breasts before looking at the valise in her hand. "Prepared as usual, I see," he said.

"Huh?"

Noting her apparent uneasiness, he chuckled inwardly. "I'm assuming you have everything you need in there to document our meetings today—paper, pens, computer. Am I right?"

M. Worthy

"Oh. Yes. I do." She smoothed her free hand over her skirt nervously. "I ... um ... I wasn't sure ..." Her voice trailed off.

"You weren't sure about what?" Damien asked calmly.

"Nothing. It's nothing."

Casually, he ran his finger along the curve of her cheek just as the elevator doors opened. "Relax, Samantha. Trust me, everything's going to be just fine."

Chapter Five

It was almost six o'clock in the evening. Samantha stood in front of the mirror in the bathroom of her hotel room. She'd removed and carefully reapplied her makeup. She'd let down her hair from the chignon she'd worn it in all day. It was freshly brushed and combed and was hanging in loose waves around her shoulders.

She'd considered taking a shower and changing her clothes, but hadn't. It didn't make much sense, since she'd brought only business suits, underwear, and the pajamas she planned to wear to bed. *At least my underwear is sexy.* Samantha blinked at her reflection. "Where is this craziness coming from? It's totally stupid," she said to the face in the mirror. *There's no reason for me to be nervous. I've known Damien for almost a year now. We're colleagues. That's all. He's never treated me with anything except the utmost courtesy.*

M. Worthy

That was true, but today was somehow different. A sexual tension had seemed to permeate the air surrounding them ever since early that morning when their gazes connected at the airport back in Philadelphia. He'd held Samantha's hand and found several excuses to touch her in the past eleven hours.

They were meeting in the hotel restaurant for dinner. Then she'd return to her room ... alone. Wouldn't she? Samantha pursed her lips. She'd applied deep red lipstick to her full mouth. *I wonder how Damien would feel about having red lipstick all over his big, hard, black cock?* The licentious thought was accompanied by the now familiar tingling between her thighs. *Where are these outrageous ideas coming from?*

Damien was watching the entrance of the dining room at the hotel. He noted that Samantha Mason was wearing the same business suit she'd had on all day. *Too bad. I'd really like to see her dressed in a tight, low-cut number that showed off those gorgeous knockers and beautiful ass.* He felt his cock jump in his pants. *We'll save that for another time. What I want most tonight is to get her out of those*

Only You

clothes. I'm going to lick, suck, and fuck her all night long. She's going to learn from personal experience why they say, "Once you go black, you never go back."

Lifting his hand, he waved to her from where he sat. He'd chosen a booth covered with a long wine colored tablecloth in the most private corner of the room. *I wonder what her pussy tastes like? Hmmm. Sounds like a most delicious dessert.* Damien put his hand over the outline of his cock. It was ten inches long and very thick. *I probably should have jacked off in the shower*, he thought as he stroked himself softly under the tablecloth. No matter. He had plenty of stamina, and he planned to use every bit of it on the lovely Miss Mason.

"Sorry if I'm late, Damien," she said as she slid into the booth across from him.

"You're not late. I got here a little early. What would you like to drink?" he asked.

"What's that you're having?

"Black Russian. Want one?"

"I've never tried one. What's it taste like?" she asked.

M. Worthy

"It's hard to describe. Here. Taste mine. See if you like it." He watched her mouth as she sipped the potent cocktail.

"Umm. That's pretty good." She nodded. "Okay. I'll have one of those."

"What do you usually drink?" Damien asked.

"I don't ... usually drink, that is."

"Oh?"

"My mom was an alcoholic. It was pretty hard on my dad and us kids. So ..." She shrugged.

"I get it. My mom doesn't drink either. I think my dad might have been an alcoholic, but I'm not sure. He was gone before I was born."

There was a look of sadness in her eyes when she said, "So you grew up without a father?"

"No. My mother married Isiah when I was seven. He was the only dad I ever knew."

"So what happened? Where is he now?"

Only You

"Heaven, I suppose. If there is such a place. Cancer. He was only in his fifties. I'm hoping Mom finds another man someday. It'll be hard for her to replace Isiah, but it's better than her spending the rest of her life alone."

"She has you."

"That's true, but there are things a woman needs that only a husband can give."

"Or a lover."

Damien raised his eyebrows. "Yes. A lover. I'll drink to that." He took a sip of his drink and flagged down the server. "The lady would like a Black Russian."

Chapter Six

By the time they finished dinner, Samantha was completely relaxed. She and Damien got along very well. They talked about work, their families, things they liked to do in their spare time. Their conversation was filled with laughter and jokes, but they also touched on more serious topics, such as politics and religion—subjects often considered taboo for a newly blossoming relationship.

"So tell me about the picture you threw in the trash can yesterday," Damien said easily. "Who was he? How long were you a couple? When did you break up?"

Samantha took another sip of her cocktail. "Jacob. Jake Forester. We met in college. I thought he was 'the one.' " She made air quotes with her fingers.

"What happened?"

Only You

"I caught him cheating on me. For all I know, it might not have been the first time he'd done it—just the first time he got caught."

"Were you engaged?"

Samantha scoffed. "Heck no. Not even close. He was the proverbial Big Man on Campus. Me? I was nobody. I never was quite sure why he chose me."

"You're *far* from a nobody, Samantha. You're one of the smartest, most beautiful women I've ever known in my life."

"Thank you, Damien, but you don't have to say things like that. I'm okay with being who I am."

"I'm not just *saying* it, Samantha. I *mean* it. I've been watching you for a long time now—ever since you came to work at the firm."

"You have?"

"Can I tell you a secret?" Damien asked.

"Sure. What is it?"

"I *asked* to have you assigned as my assistant on this trip. I wanted the chance to get to know you better."

M. Worthy

"I'm flattered, Damien. I really am. The truth is I've been having these *feelings* ... I can't really explain it."

"Did you notice anything about our rooms?"

"If you mean the adjoining door, yes, I noticed. I was wondering if ..."

"How would you feel about leaving that door open?" Damien slipped off his shoe and ran his foot up and down Samantha's leg.

"I think I'd like that," she whispered.

They held hands as they walked through the lobby to the elevator. He put his arm around her once they stepped inside. "I'm going to kiss you now, Samantha." He angled his head and placed his lips on hers. She gripped his arms and whimpered softly. When the doors of the elevator opened on their floor, her arms were wrapped around him, and her body was pressed against his.

He took her hand and led her to his room. Then he opened the door and followed her in. The sun had disappeared from the sky, and the room was dark. Damien

Only You

flipped on the switch in the bathroom leaving enough light for them to find their way around.

"Can I get you anything?" he asked.

Samantha shook her head and sat down on the small sofa. Damien sat next to her and put his arm around her shoulders. She leaned into him and nuzzled his neck.

"You smell good," she whispered.

Damien lifted her chin and looked steadily into her eyes. "You're beautiful, Samantha Mason," he said before touching his lips to hers.

Samantha realized that she *wanted* Damien in a very basic and *very* sexual way. It was something she'd never really experienced before. When he kissed her, something *happened* to her. It had never been this way—even with Jacob. For the first time in her life, she wanted to completely forget everything except this moment. She wanted to deepen their kiss. She wanted to know how it would feel to have his hands on her and to have her hands on him. She wanted him ... all of him ... every inch of him.

M. Worthy

Their kiss intensified—became like a hunger. It was as if he wanted to devour her. She loved it. She readily opened her lips to him with a sigh. A rumbling groan escaped from his throat as his tongue tangled with hers. She whimpered with pleasure and the flame of her desire ignited into an inferno.

"I want to make love to you," Damien whispered. "I want to make love to you in a way that will spoil you for any other man."

"Yes. *Please.*" She was suddenly desperate for him—for his touch on her naked skin.

Damien pulled her onto his lap. She wrapped her arms around him and threaded her fingers into his hair. When she wiggled her bottom against his already raging hard on, he felt like he was going to explode.

Pressing his mouth to hers, he then traced her lips with his tongue. When she moaned, his tongue entered her mouth, tasting her. Delicious ... slightly salty with the faintest hint of the Black Russian she'd been drinking.

Only You

Damien was an artful and accomplished lover. It was extremely important to him that the woman he was with enjoyed herself as much or more than he did. He made it his priority. He knew exactly how to turn a woman on—how to satisfy her.

Samantha's apparent need for him, and his for her, was unlike from anything he'd experienced before with anyone else. Damien was feeling something for Sam that was uniquely different. He'd been watching her from afar for such a long time. Now that he was with her in such an intimate way, stronger and deeper feelings than he'd ever felt before seemed to have awakened.

She shivered slightly as he began exploring her body with his hands. Moving from her back down to her hips, he could feel the firmness of her muscles beneath her clothes. He moved his hand down her leg. He needed to feel her skin. He needed to touch her, to feel her flesh in his hands.

Pulling his mouth away from hers, he groaned and said, "I need to see you, Sammi. All of you. Please."

M. Worthy

She didn't say a word, but took his face in her hands and kissed him deeply. Then she stood before him and stripped. Her eyes never left his as she first removed her jacket and dropped it on the floor. She then pulled the blouse she was wearing from the waistband of her skirt.

"Oh god, Sam. You're so fucking beautiful." He was hit with an amazingly strong surge of desire and lust. His erection was straining for release. He could hardly wait to bury himself into her—hard and fast. Yet somewhere a part of him wanted to allow her to be in control. He watched. He waited.

She continued to stare into his eyes. As she unbuttoned her blouse, her tongue snaked out of her mouth. She licked her lips sensuously. Next she opened the clasp on the skirt she was wearing and unzipped it. The garment fell to the floor. She stepped out of it—leaving her clad only in a lacy bra and panties.

"Come here, Sammi. I need to touch you," he whispered as he opened his arms.

Only You

Taking a deep shaking breath, she stepped toward him—straddled him. Then she rubbed her sex against him, rocking up and down. Silently she began to unbutton his shirt. As she opened each button, she followed her fingers with her teeth and tongue, licking and nipping softly.

"Samantha. Sweetheart. You're driving me crazy. I want you so bad."

She silenced him by placing her mouth on his. As she pushed the shirt off his shoulders, she rubbed her chest against his. Their eyes were locked. She watched his reaction as she rolled his nipples between her thumbs and forefinger.

Damien groaned. Reaching up he inched the thin straps of her bra from her shoulders, releasing the fullness of her breasts. "I love your tits ... they're perfect." *You're perfect.* He took them in his hands. There was no doubt—he had to have them in his mouth. He needed to find out if they tasted as delicious as they looked. *Damn. Yes.* He licked and swirled his tongue over her, sucking and teasing her nipples.

M. Worthy

His hard on was throbbing behind his zipper. Once again, he covered her mouth with his. This time their kiss was different. Now he was desperate for her. His desire had grown to a whole new level. Samantha continued to rub her sex against him and press her chest to his. "Your tits feel so damn good, Sam. I need to touch *all* of you."

She whimpered as he again filled his hands with her breasts. Her nipples puckered as he tweaked them with his thumbs. Seconds later his mouth replaced his hands once more. He swirled his tongue over her hardened nipples before lightly scraping his teeth over her aroused flesh. Sucking her nipple into his mouth, he slid his hand up her inner thigh. When he touched her panties they were damp with her arousal.

She was so sensual, so responsive. He wasn't even surprised. He instinctively knew that she would be that way. He slid his finger along her panty line and then under the thin material. She gasped audibly when his finger slid into the slick warmth between her legs.

"You're so wet, Sam. So hot and so wet for *me*. I have to taste you." He felt her stiffen slightly. Staring into her

Only You

eyes, he put his finger into his mouth. "Ummmm. Sweet ambrosia," he said as he savored her juices. He was gratified when he saw her eyes grow even darker with passion. *"More, Sammi. I want more,"* he said. He then slipped his fingers into the sides of the tiny band of lace on her hips, pulling her panties down and then off. She started to close her legs. "No," he said as he placed his hand against her thigh. "Open. Open for me, Samantha." His gaze bored into hers. Then he lowered his mouth to feast on the sweetness between her legs.

Samantha had never felt this good ... or this out of control before. Her legs were shaking, and his name fell from her lips as shock waves of pleasure moved through her body. Her hands gripped the cushions below her and then moved to his shoulders. She looked down her nearly naked body. Their eyes met and his were filled with such desire ... such passion. She gasped as he inserted two of his long, dark, tapered fingers deeply into her.

"My god, Sam. You're so tight–so wet." He moved his tongue in a circular motion around her clit as his fingers moved in and out. "Come for me, Sammi. I want to watch

M. Worthy

you explode, and I want to feel your muscles grab me when you do."

"Please. I'm not even sure if I can. I've never ...," she protested. "Besides, now I want to touch *you*. I want to taste *you*. Then I want to feel you inside me. Please."

He did as she asked without a word, but couldn't resist pushing his fingers in and out of her once more before he removed them. Then he slid up her body, pressing his rock hard erection to where his hand had been. Slowly he lowered his head to hers, parted her lips and slipped his tongue into her mouth. Because they were on his tongue, she tasted her own juices for the first time. The taste and the pleasure she felt was unexpected and most enjoyable.

Sam moved her hand to his waist, tugging on his belt. "*Please*," she begged.

He got up and stood in front of her, much like she'd stood before him earlier. She was nervous. Her hands fumbled as she tried to undo his belt and trousers as quickly as she could. Finally she got them unzipped and pushed them down over his slim hips. She gulped when she saw the

Only You

size of his erection. It was *huge*, and so dark—much darker than the rest of his body. Hesitantly, she took it in her hand, feeling the smoothness of his skin over his long, thick shaft.

"Sam," he groaned as she took him into her mouth greedily. She used one hand to continue to stroke his cock. It was so thick, the fingers of her small hand barely wrapped around it. With her other hand, she grabbed his hip. Instinctively, she wanted to take him deeper into her mouth. His buttock was firm and round in her hand, but she felt the muscles in his legs shaking. "I ... I have to sit down," he managed to say before dropping onto the coffee table in front of the sofa. Samantha continued to suck and stroke his dick, and he brushed her hair back from her face. "Oh my god, Sammi, do you have any idea what you're doing to me?" Gently he lifted her head. Leaning toward her, he smiled and once more pressed his lips to hers. "Come on," he said as he slipped his feet and legs out from his shoes and the pants crumpled beneath him. Taking her hand, he stood, pulling her up from the couch with him. "Bed," he said.

"Yes," she replied softly. "Bed."

M. Worthy

The next thing she knew, he had swept her into his arms. He walked the short distance across the room to the king-sized bed. Light from the moon streamed in through the open drapes.

Standing next to the bed with her in his arms he said, "Push the blankets down, will you please, sugar?" Releasing one of her arms from his neck, she did as he asked. He laid her tenderly down on the soft sheets. "God," he murmured, "you're so damn gorgeous." When she started to undo the clasp between her breasts, he stopped her. "Let me," he whispered. Before reaching for the fastener, he engulfed her fullness in his hands once more, kneading and stroking her hardened nipples. He followed with his mouth, licking her stiff peaks with his tongue before suckling. "Ummm," he said as he continued to suck. Finally he removed the last garment she wore.

Once she was completely naked, he lay down beside her and pulled her close. Again he covered her mouth with his. The kiss was slow and sweet, the most sensual and seductive kiss of her life. It felt as if Damien poured every ounce of his desire into it, and she drank it in.

Only You

Samantha's passion had ratcheted up to an even higher level. For once she wanted to let go completely ... to hold nothing back. She wasn't *trying* to be anyone other than herself. She was just a woman who was giving herself totally, and allowing her desires to overcome any and all reservations. Her hands caressed his body, exploring every inch. She loved the way the soft, dark skin of his shaft moved with each stroke of her hand up and down. Her body moved of its own accord. Without even knowing how it happened, she found herself straddled across one of his thighs. She pressed her sex against the strong, firm muscles of his leg. Finally, she moved again and rubbed her wetness up and down his rigid cock. She didn't even realize it, but she was making little whimpering sounds of need.

Damien reached over and pulled a condom from the table next to the bed. Taking it from him she said, "I want to do it. Please, let me." His gaze burned into her as he watched her tear the foil package with her teeth. She felt him throb and heard him groan as she rolled the soft latex over his length.

M. Worthy

When he moved on top of her, she spread her legs to allow him to position himself between her thighs. As much as she wanted to have him inside her, she also needed to kiss him again. Her arms went around his neck, and she pulled his mouth to hers. There was so much passion in their kiss, she couldn't think of anything except the feel of his lips on hers, his body crushed against her own.

She arched upward when she finally felt the head of his shaft touch the slick opening between her thighs. "Yes. *Yes,*" she whispered urgently. He slid into her slowly, filling her with his thickness and length. She relished every inch. "Oh, god. *Damien.*" He pulled back until he was almost out of her completely and then pushed back in all the way. Never before had she felt so filled or so fulfilled. She moved in rhythm with him, a dance as old as time. With every thrust she went higher and higher—coming closer and closer to experiencing her first orgasm.

"Oh, my God. I ... I think ... I think I'm ..." She threw her head back and forth as she felt her body reaching for release. *"Aaarghhhh!"* At last, it was as if fireworks exploded, and she gave into complete and total pleasure. She felt an

Only You

intense sense of gratification as her inner muscles contracted around him. Samantha heard him groan in ecstasy as they went over the edge together.

The End

Want more? Look for Book 2 in the Only Series.

Only One

www.ingramcontent.com/pod-product-compliance
Lightning Source LLC
Chambersburg PA
CBHW071222130626
46555CB00004B/1807